THE SOUL OF NICHOLAS SNYDERS, OR THE MISER OF ZANDAM

By

Jerome K. Jerome

British Library Cataloguing-in-Publication Data
A catalogue record for this book is available from the
British Library

Jerome K. Jerome

Jerome Klapka Jerome was born in Walsall, England in 1859. Both his parents died while he was in his early teens, and he was forced to quit school to support himself. Jerome worked for a number of years collecting coal along railway tracks, before trying his hand at acting, journalism, teaching and soliciting. At long last, in 1885, he had some success with *On the Stage – and Off*, a comic memoir of his experiences with an acting troupe. Jerome produced a number of essays over the following years, and married in 1888, spending the honeymoon in "a little boat" on the Thames.

In 1889, Jerome published his most successful and best-remembered work, *Three Men in a Boat*. Featuring himself and two of his friends encountering humorous situations while floating down the Thames in a small boat, the book was an instant success, and has never been out of print. In fact, its popularity was such that the number of registered Thames boats went up fifty percent in the year following its publication. With the financial security provided by *Three Men in a Boat*, Jerome was able to dedicate himself fully to writing, producing eleven more novels and a number of anthologies of short fiction.

In 1926, Jerome published his autobiography, *My Life and Times*. He died a year later, aged 68.

THE SOUL OF NICHOLAS SNYDERS, OR THE MISER OF ZANDAM

Once upon a time in Zandam, which is by the Zuider Zee, there lived a wicked man named Nicholas Snyders. He was mean and hard and cruel, and loved but one thing in the world, and that was gold. And even that not for its own sake. He loved the power gold gave him—the power to tyrannize and to oppress, the power to cause suffering at his will. They said he had no soul, but there they were wrong. All men own—or, to speak more correctly, are owned by—a soul; and the soul of Nicholas Snyders was an evil soul. He lived in the old windmill which still is standing on the quay, with only little Christina to wait upon him and keep house for him. Christina was an orphan whose parents had died in debt. Nicholas, to Christina's everlasting gratitude, had cleared their memory—it cost but a few hundred florins—in consideration that Christina should work for him without wages. Christina formed his entire household, and only one willing visitor ever darkened his door, the widow Toelast. Dame Toelast was rich and almost as great a miser as Nicholas himself. "Why should not we two marry?" Nicholas had once croaked to the widow Toelast. "Together we should be masters of all Zandam." Dame Toelast had answered with a cackling laugh; but Nicholas was never in haste.

One afternoon Nicholas Snyders sat alone at his desk in the centre of the great semi-circular room that took up half the ground floor of the windmill, and that served him for an office, and there came a knocking at the outer door.

"Come in!" cried Nicholas Snyders. He spoke in a tone quite kind for Nicholas Snyders. He felt so sure it was Jan knocking at the door—Jan Van der Voort, the young sailor, now master of his own ship, come to demand of him the hand of little Christina. In anticipation, Nicholas Snyders tasted the joy of dashing Jan's hopes to the ground; of hearing him plead, then rave; of watching the growing pallor that would overspread Jan's handsome face as Nicholas would, point by point, explain to him the consequences of defiance— how, firstly, Jan's old mother should be turned out of her home, his old father put into prison for debt; how, secondly, Jan himself should be pursued without remorse, his ship be bought over his head before he could complete the purchase. The interview would afford to Nicholas Snyders sport after his own soul. Since Jan's return the day before, he had been looking forward to it. Therefore, feeling sure it was Jan, he cried "Come in!" quite cheerily.

But it was not Jan. It was somebody Nicholas Snyders had never set eyes on before. And neither, after that one visit, did Nicholas Snyders ever set eyes upon him again. The light was fading, and Nicholas Snyders was not the man to light candles before they were needed, so that he was never able to describe with any precision the stranger's appearance. Nicholas thought he seemed an old man, but alert in all his movements; while his eyes—the one thing about him Nicholas saw with any clearness—were curiously bright and piercing.

"Who are you?" asked Nicholas Snyders, taking no pains to disguise his disappointment.

"I am a pedlar," answered the stranger. His voice was clear and not unmusical, with just the suspicion of roguishness behind.

"Not wanting anything," answered Nicholas Snyders drily. "Shut the door and be careful of the step."

But instead the stranger took a chair and drew it nearer, and, himself in shadow, looked straight into Nicholas Snyders' face and laughed.

"Are you quite sure, Nicholas Snyders? Are you quite sure there is nothing you require?"

"Nothing," growled Nicholas Snyders—"except the sight of your back." The stranger bent forward, and with his long, lean hand touched Nicholas Snyders playfully upon the knee. "Wouldn't you like a soul, Nicholas Snyders?" he asked.

"Think of it," continued the strange pedlar, before Nicholas could recover power of speech. "For forty years you have drunk the joy of being mean and cruel. Are you not tired of the taste, Nicholas Snyders? Wouldn't you like a change? Think of it, Nicholas Snyders—the joy of being loved, of hearing yourself blessed, instead of cursed! Wouldn't it be good fun, Nicholas Snyders—just by way of a change? If you don't like it, you can return and be yourself again."

What Nicholas Snyders, recalling all things afterwards, could never understand was why he sat there, listening in patience to the stranger's talk; for, at the time, it seemed to him the jesting of a wandering fool. But something about the stranger had impressed him.

"I have it with me," continued the odd pedlar; "and as for price—" The stranger made a gesture indicating dismissal of all sordid details. "I look for my reward in watching the result of the experiment. I am something of a philosopher. I take an interest in these matters. See." The stranger dived between his legs and produced from his pack a silver flask of cunning workmanship and laid it on the table.

"Its flavour is not unpleasant," explained the stranger. "A little bitter; but one does not drink it by the goblet: a wineglassful, such as one would of old Tokay, while the mind of both is fixed on the same thought: 'May my soul pass into him, may his pass into me!' The operation is quite simple: the secret lies within the drug." The stranger patted the quaint flask as though it had been some little dog.

"You will say: 'Who will exchange souls with Nicholas Snyders?'" The stranger appeared to have come prepared with an answer to all questions. "My friend, you are rich; you need not fear. It is the possession men value the least of all they have. Choose your soul and drive your bargain. I leave that to you with one word of counsel only: you will find the young readier than the old—the young, to whom the world promises all things for gold. Choose you a fine, fair, fresh, young soul, Nicholas Snyders; and choose it quickly. Your hair is somewhat grey, my friend. Taste, before you die, the joy of living."

The strange pedlar laughed and, rising, closed his pack. Nicholas Snyders neither moved nor spoke, until with the soft clanging of the massive door his senses returned to him. Then, seizing the flask the stranger had left behind him, he sprang from his chair, meaning to fling it after him into the street. But the flashing of the firelight on its burnished surface stayed his hand.

"After all, the case is of value," Nicholas chuckled, and put the flask aside and, lighting the two tall candles, buried himself again in his green-bound ledger. Yet still from time to time Nicholas Snyders' eye would wander to where the silver flask remained half hidden among dusty papers. And later there came again a knocking at the door, and this time it really was young Jan who entered.

Jan held out his great hand across the littered desk.

"We parted in anger, Nicholas Snyders. It was my fault. You were in the right. I ask you to forgive me. I was poor. It was selfish of me to wish the little maid to share with me my poverty. But now I am no longer poor."

"Sit down," responded Nicholas in kindly tone. "I have heard of it. So now you are master and the owner of your ship—your very own."

"My very own after one more voyage," laughed Jan. "I have Burgomaster Allart's promise."

"A promise is not a performance," hinted Nicholas. "Burgomaster Allart is not a rich man; a higher bid might tempt him. Another might step in between you and become the owner."

Jan only laughed. "Why, that would be the work of an enemy, which, God be praised, I do not think that I possess."

"Lucky lad!" commented Nicholas; "so few of us are without enemies. And your parents, Jan, will they live with you?"

"We wished it," answered Jan, "both Christina and I. But the mother is feeble. The old mill has grown into her life."

"I can understand," agreed Nicholas. "The old vine torn from the old wall withers. And your father, Jan; people will gossip. The mill is paying?"

Jan shook his head. "It never will again; and the debts haunt him. But all that, as I tell him, is a thing of the past. His creditors have agreed to look to me and wait."

"All of them?" queried Nicholas.

"All of them I could discover," laughed Jan.

Nicholas Snyders pushed back his chair and looked at Jan with a smile upon his wrinkled face. "And so you and Christina have arranged it all?"

"With your consent, sir," answered Jan.

"You will wait for that?" asked Nicholas.

"We should like to have it, sir." Jan smiled, but the tone of his voice fell agreeably on Nicholas Snyders' ear. Nicholas Snyders loved best beating the dog that, growled and showed its teeth.

"Better not wait for that," said Nicholas Snyders. "You might have to wait long."

Jan rose, an angry flush upon his face. "So nothing changes you, Nicholas Snyders. Have it your own way, then."

"You will marry her in spite of me?"

"In spite of you and of your friends the fiends, and of your master the Devil!" flung out Jan. For Jan had a soul that was generous and brave and tender and excessively short-tempered. Even the best of souls have their failings.

"I am sorry," said old Nicholas.

"I am glad to hear it," answered Jan.

"I am sorry for your mother," explained Nicholas. "The poor dame, I fear, will be homeless in her old age. The mortgage shall be foreclosed, Jan, on your wedding-day. I am sorry for your father, Jan. His creditors, Jan— you have overlooked just one. I am sorry for him, Jan. Prison has always been his dread. I am sorry even for you, my young friend. You will have to begin life over again. Burgomaster Allart is in the hollow of my hand. I have but to say the word, your ship is mine. I wish you joy of your bride, my young friend. You must love her very dearly—you will be paying a high price for her."

It was Nicholas Snyders' grin that maddened Jan. He sought for something that, thrown straight at the wicked mouth, should silence it, and by chance his hand lighted on the pedlar's silver flask. In the same instance Nicholas Snyders' hand had closed upon it also. The grin had died away.

"Sit down," commanded Nicholas Snyders. "Let us talk further." And there was that in his voice that compelled the younger man's obedience.

"You wonder, Jan, why I seek always anger and hatred. I wonder at times myself. Why do generous thoughts never come to me, as to other men! Listen, Jan; I am in a whimsical mood. Such things cannot be, but it is a whim of mine to think it might have been. Sell me your soul, Jan, sell me your soul, that I, too, may taste this love and gladness that I hear about. For a little while, Jan, only for a little while, and I will give you all you desire."

The old man seized his pen and wrote.

"See, Jan, the ship is yours beyond mishap; the mill goes free; your father may hold up his head again. And all I ask, Jan, is that you drink to me, willing the while that your soul may go from you and become the soul of old Nicholas Snyders—for a little while, Jan, only for a little while."

With feverish hands the old man had drawn the stopper from the pedlar's flagon, had poured the wine into twin glasses. Jan's inclination was to laugh, but the old man's eagerness was almost frenzy. Surely he was mad; but that would not make less binding the paper he had signed. A true man does not jest with his soul, but the face of Christina was shining down on Jan from out the gloom.

"You will mean it?" whispered Nicholas Snyders.

"May my soul pass from me and enter into Nicholas Snyders!" answered Jan, replacing his empty glass upon the table. And the two stood looking for a moment into one another's eyes.

And the high candles on the littered desk flickered and went out, as though a breath had blown them, first one and then the other.

"I must be getting home," came the voice of Jan from the darkness. "Why did you blow out the candles?"

"We can light them again from the fire," answered Nicholas. He did not add that he had meant to ask that same question of Jan. He thrust them among the glowing logs, first one and then the other; and the shadows crept back into their corners.

"You will not stop and see Christina?" asked Nicholas.

"Not to-night," answered Jan.

"The paper that I signed," Nicholas reminded him—"you have it?"

"I had forgotten it," Jan answered.

The old man took it from the desk and handed it to him. Jan thrust it into his pocket and went out. Nicholas bolted the door behind him and returned to his desk; sat long there, his elbow resting on the open ledger.

Nicholas pushed the ledger aside and laughed. "What foolery! As if such things could be! The fellow must have bewitched me."

Nicholas crossed to the fire and warmed his hands before the blaze. "Still, I am glad he is going to marry the little lass. A good lad, a good lad."

Nicholas must have fallen asleep before the fire. When he opened his eyes, it was to meet the grey dawn. He felt cold, stiff, hungry, and decidedly cross. Why had not Christina woke him up and given him his supper. Did she think he had intended to pass the night on a wooden chair? The girl was an idiot. He would go upstairs and tell her through the door just what he thought of her.

His way upstairs led through the kitchen. To his astonishment, there sat Christina, asleep before the burnt-out grate.

"Upon my word," muttered Nicholas to himself, "people in this house don't seem to know what beds are for!"

But it was not Christina, so Nicholas told himself. Christina had the look of a frightened rabbit: it had always irritated him. This girl, even in her sleep, wore an impertinent expression—a delightfully impertinent expression. Besides, this girl was pretty—marvellously pretty. Indeed, so pretty a girl Nicholas had never seen in all his life before. Why had the girls, when Nicholas was young, been so entirely different! A sudden bitterness seized Nicholas: it was as though he had just learnt that long ago, without knowing it, he had been robbed.

The child must be cold. Nicholas fetched his fur-lined cloak and wrapped it about her.

There was something else he ought to do. The idea came to him while drawing the cloak around her shoulders, very gently, not to disturb her—something he wanted to do, if only he could think what it was. The girl's lips were parted. She appeared to be speaking to him, asking him to do this thing—or telling him not to do it. Nicholas could not be sure which. Half a dozen times he turned away, and half a dozen times stole back to where she sat sleeping with that delightfully impertinent expression on her face, her lips parted. But what she wanted, or what it was he wanted, Nicholas could not think.

Perhaps Christina would know. Perhaps Christina would know who she was and how she got there. Nicholas climbed the stairs, swearing at them for creaking.

Christina's door was open. No one was in the room; the bed had not been slept upon. Nicholas descended the creaking stairs.

The girl was still asleep. Could it be Christina herself? Nicholas examined the delicious features one by one. Never before, so far as he could recollect, had he seen the girl; yet around her neck—Nicholas had not noticed it before—lay Christina's locket, rising and falling as she breathed. Nicholas knew it well; the one thing belonging to her mother Christina had insisted on keeping. The one thing about which she had ever defied him. She would never have parted with that locket. It must be Christina herself. But what had happened to her? Or to himself. Remembrance rushed in upon him. The odd pedlar! The scene with Jan! But surely all that had been a dream? Yet there upon the littered desk still stood the pedlar's silver flask, together with the twin stained glasses.

Nicholas tried to think, but his brain was in a whirl. A ray of sunshine streaming through the window fell across the dusty room. Nicholas had never seen the sun, that he could recollect. Involuntarily he stretched his hands towards it, felt a pang of grief when it vanished, leaving only the grey light. He drew the rusty bolts, flung open the great door. A strange world lay before him, a new world of lights and shadows, that wooed him with their beauty—a world of low, soft voices that called to him. There came to him again that bitter sense of having been robbed.

"I could have been so happy all these years," murmured old Nicholas to himself. "It is just the little town I could have loved—so quaint, so quiet, so homelike. I might have had friends, old cronies, children of my own maybe—"

A vision of the sleeping Christina flashed before his eyes. She had come to him a child, feeling only gratitude towards him. Had he had eyes with which to see her, all things might have been different.

Was it too late? He is not so old—not so very old. New life is in his veins. She still loves Jan, but that was the Jan of yesterday. In the future, Jan's every word and deed will be prompted by the evil soul that was once the soul of Nicholas Snyders—that Nicholas Snyders remembers well. Can any woman love that, let the case be as handsome as you will?

Ought he, as an honest man, to keep the soul he had won from Jan by what might be called a trick? Yes, it had been a fair bargain, and Jan had taken his price. Besides, it was not as if Jan had fashioned his own soul; these things are chance. Why should one man be given gold, and another be given parched peas? He has as much right to Jan's soul as Jan ever had. He is wiser, he can do more good with it. It was Jan's soul that loved Christina; let Jan's soul win her if it can. And Jan's soul, listening to the argument, could not think of a word to offer in opposition.

Christina was still asleep when Nicholas re-entered the kitchen. He lighted the fire and cooked the breakfast and then aroused her gently. There was no doubt it was Christina. The moment her eyes rested on old Nicholas, there came back to her the frightened rabbit look that had always irritated him. It irritated him now, but the irritation was against himself.

"You were sleeping so soundly when I came in last night—" Christina commenced.

"And you were afraid to wake me," Nicholas interrupted her. "You thought the old curmudgeon would be cross. Listen, Christina. You paid off yesterday the last debt your father owed. It was to an old sailor—I had not been able to find him before. Not a cent more do you owe, and there remains to you, out of your wages, a hundred florins. It is yours whenever you like to ask me for it."

Christina could not understand, neither then nor during the days that followed; nor did Nicholas enlighten her. For the soul of Jan had entered into a very wise old man, who knew that the best way to live down the past is to live boldly the present. All that Christina could be sure of was that the old Nicholas Snyders had mysteriously vanished, that in his place remained a new Nicholas, who looked at her with kindly eyes—frank and honest, compelling confidence. Though Nicholas never said so, it came to Christina that she herself, her sweet example, her ennobling influence it was that had wrought this wondrous change. And to Christina the explanation seemed not impossible—seemed even pleasing.

The sight of his littered desk was hateful to him. Starting early in the morning, Nicholas would disappear for the entire day, returning in the evening tired but cheerful, bringing with him flowers that Christina laughed at, telling him they were weeds. But what mattered names? To Nicholas they were beautiful. In Zandam the children ran from him, the dogs barked after him. So Nicholas, escaping through byways, would wander far into the country. Children in the villages around came to know a kind old fellow who loved to linger, his hands resting on his staff, watching their play, listening to their laughter; whose ample pockets were storehouses of good things. Their elders, passing by, would whisper to one another how like he was in features to wicked old Nick, the miser of Zandam, and would wonder where he came from. Nor was it only the faces of the children that taught his lips to smile. It troubled him at first to find the world so full of marvellously pretty girls—of pretty women also, all more or less lovable. It bewildered him. Until he found that, notwithstanding, Christina remained always in his thoughts the prettiest, the most lovable of them all. Then every pretty face rejoiced him: it reminded him of Christina.

On his return the second day, Christina had met him with sadness in her eyes. Farmer Beerstraater, an old friend of her father's, had called to see Nicholas; not finding Nicholas, had talked a little with Christina. A hardhearted creditor was turning him out of his farm. Christina pretended not to know that the creditor was Nicholas himself, but marvelled that such wicked men could be. Nicholas said nothing, but the next day Farmer Beerstraater had called again, all smiles, blessings, and great wonder.

"But what can have come to him?" repeated Farmer Beerstraater over and over.

Christina had smiled and answered that perhaps the good God had touched his heart; but thought to herself that perhaps it had been the good influence of another. The tale flew. Christina found herself besieged on every hand, and, finding her intercessions invariably successful, grew day by day more pleased with herself, and by consequence more pleased with Nicholas Snyders. For Nicholas was a cunning old gentleman. Jan's soul in him took delight in undoing the evil the soul of Nicholas had wrought. But the brain of Nicholas Snyders that remained to him whispered: "Let the little maid think it is all her doing."

The news reached the ears of Dame Toelast. The same evening saw her seated in the inglenook opposite Nicholas Snyders, who smoked and seemed bored.

"You are making a fool of yourself, Nicholas Snyders," the Dame told him. "Everybody is laughing at you."

"I had rather they laughed than cursed me," growled Nicholas.

"Have you forgotten all that has passed between us?" demanded the Dame.

"Wish I could," sighed Nicholas.

"At your age—" commenced the Dame.

"I am feeling younger than I ever felt in all my life," Nicholas interrupted her.

"You don't look it," commented the Dame.

"What do looks matter?" snapped Nicholas. "It is the soul of a man that is the real man."

"They count for something, as the world goes," explained the Dame. "Why, if I liked to follow your example and make a fool of myself, there are young men, fine young men, handsome young men—"

"Don't let me stand in your way," interposed Nicholas quickly. "As you say, I am old and I have a devil of a temper. There must be many better men than I am, men more worthy of you."

"I don't say there are not," returned the Dame: "but nobody more suitable. Girls for boys, and old women for old men. I haven't lost my wits, Nicholas Snyders, if you have. When you are yourself again—"

Nicholas Snyders sprang to his feet. "I am myself," he cried, "and intend to remain myself! Who dares say I am not myself?"

"I do," retorted the Dame with exasperating coolness. "Nicholas Snyders is not himself when at the bidding of a pretty-faced doll he flings his money out of the window with both hands. He is a creature bewitched, and I am sorry for him. She'll fool you for the sake of her friends till you haven't a cent left, and then she'll laugh at you. When you are yourself, Nicholas Snyders, you will be crazy with yourself—remember that." And Dame Toelast marched out and slammed the door behind her.

"Girls for boys, and old women for old men." The phrase kept ringing in his ears. Hitherto his new-found happiness had filled his life, leaving no room for thought. But the old Dame's words had sown the seed of reflection.

Was Christina fooling him? The thought was impossible. Never once had she pleaded for herself, never once for Jan. The evil thought was the creature of Dame Toelast's evil mind. Christina loved him. Her face brightened at his coming. The fear of him had gone out of her; a pretty tyranny had replaced it. But was it the love that he sought? Jan's soul in old Nick's body was young and ardent. It desired Christina not as a daughter, but as a wife. Could it win her in spite of old Nick's body? The soul of Jan was an impatient soul. Better to know than to doubt.

"Do not light the candles; let us talk a little by the light of the fire only," said Nicholas. And Christina, smiling, drew her chair towards the blaze. But Nicholas sat in the shadow.

"You grow more beautiful every day, Christina," said Nicholas-"sweeter and more womanly. He will be a happy man who calls you wife."

The smile passed from Christina's face. "I shall never marry," she answered. "Never is a long word, little one."

"A true woman does not marry the man she does not love."

"But may she not marry the man she does?" smiled Nicholas.

"Sometimes she may not," Christina explained.

"And when is that?"

Christina's face was turned away. "When he has ceased to love her."

The soul in old Nick's body leapt with joy. "He is not worthy of you, Christina. His new fortune has changed him. Is it not so? He thinks only of money. It is as though the soul of a miser had entered into him. He would marry even Dame Toelast for the sake of her gold-bags and her broad lands and her many mills, if only she would have him. Cannot you forget him?"

"I shall never forget him. I shall never love another man. I try to hide it; and often I am content to find there is so much in the world that I can do. But my heart is breaking." She rose and, kneeling beside him, clasped her hands around him. "I am glad you have let me tell you," she said. "But for you I could not have borne it. You are so good to me."

For answer he stroked with his withered hand the golden hair that fell disordered about his withered knees. She raised her eyes to him; they were filled with tears, but smiling.

"I cannot understand," she said. "I think sometimes that you and he must have changed souls. He is hard and mean and cruel, as you used to be." She laughed, and the arms around him tightened for a moment. "And now you are kind and tender and great, as once he was. It is as if the good God had taken away my lover from me to give to me a father."

"Listen to me, Christina," he said. "It is the soul that is the man, not the body. Could you not love me for my new soul?"

"But I do love you," answered Christina, smiling through her tears.

"Could you as a husband?" The firelight fell upon her face. Nicholas, holding it between his withered hands, looked into it long and hard; and reading what he read there, laid it back against his breast and soothed it with his withered hand.

"I was jesting, little one," he said. "Girls for boys, and old women for old men. And so, in spite of all, you still love Jan?"

"I love him," answered Christina. "I cannot help it."

"And if he would, you would marry him, let his soul be what it may?"

"I love him," answered Christina. "I cannot help it."

Old Nicholas sat alone before the dying fire. Is it the soul or the body that is the real man? The answer was not so simple as he had thought it.

"Christina loved Jan"—so Nicholas mumbled to the dying fire—"when he had the soul of Jan. She loves him still, though he has the soul of Nicholas Snyders. When I asked her if she could love me, it was terror I read in her eyes, though Jan's soul is now in me; she divined it. It must be the body that is the real Jan, the real Nicholas. If the soul of Christina entered into the body of Dame Toelast, should I turn from Christina, from her golden hair, her fathomless eyes, her asking lips, to desire the shrivelled carcass of Dame Toelast? No; I should still shudder at the thought of her. Yet when I had the soul of Nicholas Snyders, I did not loathe her, while Christina was naught to me. It must be with the soul that we love, else Jan would still love Christina and I should be Miser Nick. Yet here am I loving Christina, using Nicholas Snyders' brain and gold to thwart Nicholas Snyders' every scheme, doing everything that I know will make him mad when he comes back into his own body; while Jan cares no longer for Christina, would marry Dame Toelast for her broad lands, her many mills. Clearly it is the soul that is the real man. Then ought I not to be glad, thinking I am going back into my own body, knowing that I shall wed Christina? But I am not glad; I am very miserable. I shall not go with Jan's soul, I feel it; my own soul will come back to me. I shall be again the hard, cruel, mean old man I was before, only now I shall be poor and helpless. The folks will laugh at me, and I shall curse them, powerless to do them evil. Even Dame Toelast will not want me when she learns all. And yet I must do this thing. So long as Jan's soul is in me, I love

Christina better than myself. I must do this for her sake. I love her—I cannot help it."

Old Nicholas rose, took from the place, where a month before he had hidden it, the silver flask of cunning workmanship.

"Just two more glassfuls left," mused Nicholas, as he gently shook the flask against his ear. He laid it on the desk before him, then opened once again the old green ledger, for there still remained work to be done.

He woke Christina early. "Take these letters, Christina," he commanded. "When you have delivered them all, but not before, go to Jan; tell him I am waiting here to see him on a matter of business." He kissed her and seemed loth to let her go.

"I shall only be a little while," smiled Christina.

"All partings take but a little while," he answered.

Old Nicholas had foreseen the trouble he would have. Jan was content, had no desire to be again a sentimental young fool, eager to saddle himself with a penniless wife. Jan had other dreams.

"Drink, man, drink!" cried Nicholas impatiently, "before I am tempted to change my mind. Christina, provided you marry her, is the richest bride in Zandam. There is the deed; read it; and read quickly."

Then Jan consented, and the two men drank. And there passed a breath between them as before; and Jan with his hands covered his eyes a moment.

It was a pity, perhaps, that he did so, for in that moment Nicholas snatched at the deed that lay beside Jan on the desk. The next instant it was blazing in the fire.

"Not so poor as you thought!" came the croaking voice of Nicholas. "Not so poor as you thought! I can build again, I can build again!" And the creature, laughing hideously, danced with its withered arms spread out before the blaze, lest Jan should seek to rescue Christina's burning dowry before it was destroyed.

Jan did not tell Christina. In spite of all Jan could say, she would go back. Nicholas Snyders drove her from the door with curses. She could not understand. The only thing clear was that Jan had come back to her.

"'Twas a strange madness that seized upon me," Jan explained. "Let the good sea breezes bring us health."

So from the deck of Jan's ship they watched old Zandam till it vanished into air.

Christina cried a little at the thought of never seeing it again; but Jan comforted her and later new faces hid the old.

And old Nicholas married Dame Toelast, but, happily, lived to do evil only for a few years longer.

Long after, Jan told Christina the whole story, but it sounded very improbable, and Christina—though, of course, she did not say so—did not quite believe it, but thought Jan was trying to explain away that strange month of his life during which he had wooed Dame Toelast. Yet it certainly was strange that Nicholas, for the same short month, had been so different from his usual self.

"Perhaps," thought Christina, "if I had not told him I loved Jan, he would not have gone back to his old ways. Poor old gentleman! No doubt it was despair."